For Sam, whose first word was "Please." -bb
For Mum and Dad, Thank you! -rw

Little ✹ BOOST

is published by
Picture Window Books
A Capstone Imprint
1710 Roe Crest Drive
North Mankato, Minnesota 56003
www.capstonepub.com

Library of Congress Cataloging-in-Publication data
is available on the Library of Congress website.

ISBN 978-1-4048-7419-0

Designer: Kay Fraser

Printed in China.
102011
006443

BURP!

TERRIBLE, AWFUL, HORRIBLE MANNERS!

BY BETH BRACKEN

ILLUSTRATED BY RICHARD WATSON

PICTURE WINDOW BOOKS
a capstone imprint

Once there was a boy named Pete who had terrible, awful, horrible manners.

He burped. Everywhere.

He tooted. A lot.

He picked his nose.

He didn't wash his hands.

He talked with his mouth full.

And worst of all, he never said "Thank you!"
or "Please?" or "You're welcome." Ever.

Not even to his grandma.

Pete had terrible, awful, horrible manners.

But he didn't care. He thought it was funny.
It made people look at him, and Pete enjoyed
the extra attention.

Then one night at dinner, Pete noticed
that something strange was going on.

His dad was burping. A lot. After every bite.

BURP!

"You keep burping, but you haven't said 'Excuse me,'" Pete said.

His mom tooted. Loudly. All through the meal.

"Pee-ew! Tooting is rude," Pete said.

The baby picked her nose. Maybe she didn't know any better, but nobody stopped her or told her it was gross.

"Mom! Dad! The baby keeps picking her nose,"
Pete reported. But no one said a word.

It was a strange dinnertime. Nobody said "Thank you!" or "Please?" or "You're welcome." Everyone kept burping and talking with their mouths full.

Dad even started eating with his hands!

Finally, Pete had had enough.

"How come everybody's acting so weird?"
he asked.

"I don't know what you mean," Mom said
as she wiped her nose on her sleeve.

"Yeah," Dad said. "We're just acting like you do."

Pete looked at himself. His hands were dirty, there was food all over his clothes, and he was pretty sure he had just tooted.

"Maybe I should try to use better manners," he said.

"Finally!" Dad said.
"Thank goodness," Mom said.
The baby just smiled.

"Well then," Mom said. "Let's eat!"

"Give me those vegetables!" Pete yelled.

Mom, Dad, and the baby all looked at him with surprise.

"Please?" Pete added quietly with a smile.

After that, Pete tried very hard to use his manners.

Well . . . most of the time.